J.C. HULSEY BOOKS

THE PISTOL PREACHER

J.C. HULSEY

INTRODUCTION

The Pistol Preacher 36 years old, long straight hair
Patch over left eye makes his left side blind.

Very fast and dangerous Gunfighter/Bounty Hunter

Has nightmares about when his wife died

People won't let him retire

Always somebody bracing him

He doesn't want to kill anymore, but they leave him no choice.

He preaches Sunday mornings with a six gun laying beside the Bible on the pulpit

Not married, but was married at a young age. Wife killed by renegades

Wife's killing turned him into Bounty Hunter.

Now retired, travels from town to town preaching about the love of God to any and all that will listen.

It's a hard road to travel always checking your back trail only to find that trouble is waiting for you when you arrive at your destination.

CHAPTER ONE

Crippled Jaw, Texas 1885

I was twenty two years old when my wife and unborn baby were killed. I was injured badly and almost died.

Shelley was sixteen years old when I married her. I was going on eighteen. She was the most beautiful creature I ever laid eyes on. Silky red hair hanging to her shoulders. Emerald green eyes that could melt me when she fluttered her eyelashes at me. Standing an even five feet to my six feet seemed an unlikely match, but we fit together perfectly. We had been happily married for almost four years when our perfect world was destroyed. We had just learned she was pregnant with our first child. We were sitting at the table drinking some of our homemade peach juice, when the door crashed open. I was knocked to the floor and held there by a weasel faced man and a man dressed all in black. The leader of the group, a young man, grabbed Shelly by her beautiful hair and dragged her over to the bed. A big fat Mexican sat in one of the chairs watching. I tried to get up, but it was impossible to move. The weasel faced man held a gun against my head. I heard him pull the hammer back. Shelley wasn't making as much noise as she had been.

The young leader came over and said, "Your turn, Rascal." Weasel face holstered his gun and stood. I started to struggle again and the leader fell on top of my body, knocking the wind from me. I was still trying to catch my breath when Weasel came back.

"Your turn Blackie. Man, she's a sweet one." He drew his pistol again, cocked it and placed it against the side of my head. The leader turned my head so I could see the bed. Shelley wasn't moving as Blackie climbed on top of her. The fat Mexican was just sitting there, a blank look of unconcern on his face.

"Hold her up when you're through." Blackie climbed off her, grabbed her hair and jerked her up. Her beautiful eyes weren't seeing anything.

"Hold her still." He pulled back the hammer on his pistol and squeezed the trigger. Her head snapped back and she fell onto the bed. When they killed her, it ripped a hole in my heart as big as the ocean.

"Lift up the pilgrim. It's his turn."

"You sorry SOB. I'll kill all of you." I felt it then. It felt like a mule kicked me in my chest and then a hot burning sensation as the back of my head connected with the cabin floor. Then nothing as the blackness enveloped me.

CHAPTER TWO

"Don't struggle. I know it hurts, but try not to fight. I think you might make it after I dug that slug outa you. Just relax and take up easy. No. Don't fight."

I could barely hear his voice. I was far away and couldn't find my way. I was lost in a thick fog. I needed help to get out of it. I heard the voice again, far off. If I could get closer, maybe the voice could help. Everything is circling round and round. I'm sinking into the fog again. Help! Help me! Somebody please help me?

When the fog began to clear, I could see their faces laughing, taunting me, and daring me to do something. Then I would see Shelly holding our unborn child in her arms. She would reach out for me to take the child, but I couldn't reach them. Then the fog would return. Swimming round and round. I couldn't catch hold of anything. The faces of those four men burned into my brain. I couldn't forget them if I tried. The young one that was in charge, then the one dressed all in black, he was second in command. The third man that looked like a weasel, always laughing. And the old fat Mexican who didn't want any part of it, but didn't try to stop them. He just sat and watched.

A friend of Cotton Buchanan, named Gunther Hunsaker, found me and took me to Buchanan's home where Buchanan and his daughter nursed me back to health. I was more dead than alive. How I held on as long as I did is a question I can't answer. Maybe it's because I wasn't going to let that scum get away with what they did. Hunsaker built a travois to carry me. Buchanan and his daughter met us at the door.

"Bring him inside and put him in Jesse's room. Take it easy now, he don't look none too good. Let me take a look. Yep, that bullet's got to come out. Denise, get me some whiskey and hot water. And some towels. Gunther, you hold him down so's he don't move around."

The pain was almost as bad as being shot, then I lost consciousness.

"He's waking up, Pa."

The voice of a woman, a young woman far away. Then the deeper voice of a man. I tried to see, but the fog was surrounding me again, keeping my eyes from focusing.

"Here's a little bit of water." He reached behind my head and lifted so I could swallow.

"Not too much now. As weak as you are, you need to go slow with everything. He only gave me enough to want more. My mouth felt like it was full of cotton.

"I'll give you some more later. Now, you just rest. That's what will do you the most good. Close your eyes and rest. Don't worry about anything. You're safe now."

It was as if his voice was hypnotizing me. I couldn't keep my eyes open. At least the fog seemed to be going away. I did, however, dream again about Shelly and our unborn baby. She kept trying to get me to take him from her, but I couldn't reach far enough. I would also, see the face of another young woman. I couldn't make her out, but I knew she was there. With the fog almost gone, I could see their faces laughing, taunting me daring me to do something. Then the fog would return. Swimming round and round. I couldn't catch hold of anything. Then I would see the faces of the four killers. One at a time. Each of them were laying on the ground bleeding from my bullets. The faces of those four men were burned into my brain. I couldn't forget them even if I tried.

I opened my eyes slowly, trying to look around to see where I was. Then the realization of where I was and what had happened hit me. I wanted to cry, but the tears wouldn't come. Maybe the loss of blood had dried me up. I opened my eyes.

A gray haired man with a neatly trimmed beard, in a rumpled shirt and vest with a string tie, was looking down at me.

"It's good to see you're awake. It was touch and go there for a while. You're either very lucky or very blessed. That's for sure. I had a hard time digging that slug out. An inch in either direction, you wouldn't be here. You feel like trying a little broth? It don't taste real good, but it's what you need to heal. No. Don't try to get up. You're too weak for that. Just take it easy and get some broth in your belly. Denise'll help you. She's got lots of experience helping folks."

So, her name was Denise. She had fair skin with a sprinkling of freckles across her nose, bright green eyes under a head of auburn hair, pulled into a chignon. I would like to have seen it down and flowing around her face and shoulders. She was wearing a simple blue cotton dress. On her it looked like she was dressed in a fancy ball gown.

She brought some broth in a bowl and fed me. I felt like a baby with her having to feed me with a spoon. The broth was like the man had said. It wasn't very good.

"Just a little more and then you need to rest. I'll be back later to check on you."

I would drift in and out of consciousness. Each time I awoke, Denise was either standing over me or sitting in a rocking chair at the foot of the bed.

"You're looking a lot better this morning. If you feel like sitting up, I'll shave you. You got quite a growth there. It's probably scratching you."

I sat up with her help. She carried a bowl of water and placed it on the little table by the bed. She lathered my face and started to shave my face.

"There now, that's much better. I don't particularly care for beards. Although Pa does have one."

"Thanks for shaving me, but I think I'll grow a beard even though you don't approve. I kind of like the way your father looks with his. Is there any more of that broth?"

I woke from a troubled sleep and the old man was sitting where Denise usually sat.

"Well now. You're awake. Name's Cotton. Cotton Buchanan. I'm Denise's Pa. You feel like you wanta get out of bed today?"

I tried to sit up and was pushed back against the mattress from the pain in my chest.

"I didn't mean for you to try it by yourself. I'll help you. Now, let me take your arms. Ready? Come on up. That's good. How you feeling?"

"Like a horse kicked me in the middle of my chest."

"That's normal. So, you're ok."

I swung my legs over the side of the bed. My head started swimming. If Cotton hadn't been holding onto me, I believe I would have fallen off the bed.

"Relax. Don't try to hurry. You was hurt bad and it's gonna take time for your body to heal. When you're ready, you can try to stand."

With his help I stood. I lasted maybe three, four seconds and I fell back to the bed.

"You done real good for your first time. We'll try again later. Now, lay back and rest."

"You said your name was Cotton Buchanan, the famous gunfighter? I heard he got killed in Laredo."

"Don't believe in rumors, never are accurate. I only been in Laredo one time and then I was only passing through. Stopped to water my horse, then rode out. Don't put no store in rumors. Rumors can get you in trouble. I told you my name. What's yours?"

"Clint Bowers. Did someone bury Shelly, my wife?"

"Son, there wasn't anything to bury. Those men torched your cabin when they left. How you got clear is a wonder to us all. Do you know how you got out?"

"The last thing I remember is my face hitting the floor."

"You must have been running on instinct. Apparently you wanted to live bad enough that you kept breathing. Gunther said he found you face down, by that little creek, behind the cabin. Like I said before, you're either lucky or blessed. If he hadn't come along when he did. Well, you can guess the rest."

"I can't thank you enough for what you done for me."

"No thanks necessary. Just glad you made it. Now you rest and get better."

"Can I ask another question?"

"Sure. Ask away. I can't promise I got an answer, but go ahead."

"What is Cotton Buchanan doing in a cabin in the middle of nowhere?"

"I'm retired. Doctor told me I had consumption and only got a few months to live. I wanted to spend it with my daughter. I didn't get here soon enough for my wife."

"I'm sorry to hear that. I hope the doc's wrong."

"Not likely, but thanks. Now you rest. We kept trying to stand twice a day for quite a spell until I could stand without any help.

"The next thing to do is walk. You figger you can walk?"

"I sure aim to try."

CHAPTER THREE

"I got this here cane Gunther made out of a tree limb. You can lean on it. It'll help you keep your balance."

"Thanks and tell Gunther thanks. It seems like I owe a lot to all of you."

The cane was a lot of help. Before long I was able to walk without it. I continued to get better each day.

One night after I was up and about, Denise came back from town crying.

"What's wrong, Denise? Did something happen in town?"

"It's really nothing. A couple of men said some bad things to me. That's all. They called me all kinds of names. I ran home as fast as I could."

We heard horses in the front yard.

"Hey, Red. Come on out. We wasn't through talking to you. We can make you real happy if you'll just come out."

I blew the lamp out and told Denise and Cotton to stay down.

"Let me handle this. This is my kind of thing."

"Give me your gun, Cotton. I need to do this. I owe it to you."

"Whatever you feel you owe doesn't include getting yourself killed."

"I don't plan on getting killed. I done some practicing with a gun more than a few times. Please let me do this?"

He walked over and took his holster off the peg by the fireplace.

"You sure about this?"

"I'm sure. Don't worry. They're just a couple of punks that need to be put in their place. I won't shoot unless they make me."

I put on the gun belt. I checked to make sure the pistol was loaded.

I reached down and tied the holster's thong around my leg. I straightened back up and walked to the front door. I opened it and stepped through, immediately stepping to the right. Just then, the moon moved from behind the clouds, casting a brilliant light over the scene.

"Who're you? This ain't no business of yours. You better run along if you don't want to get hurt."

"That redhead you keep calling for isn't coming out. I'm here in her place. If you've got anything more to say, you'll have to say it to me. How about it? You got some more to say?"

The slug from my gun slammed into his body, knocking him out of the saddle, his gun slipping from his unresponsive hand, and threw him into his partner, almost knocking him to the ground.

"You sorry SOB, you killed my brother. You're a dead man." He jumped from his horse and threw himself to the ground, rolling as he shot. The horses scattered from the gunshots.

One of his shots nicked my shirt sleeve. I dove behind his dead brother and shot at him. It wasn't much cover so I rolled to my right and placed two shots into the ground in front of him. He grabbed at his eyes, trying to clear the dirt from them. I stood and aimed right at him. He was bringing his weapon up when the bullet from my gun caught him. He threw his gun into the air and grabbed at his throat, trying to stop the blood from leaving his body. He slumped to the ground, making a gurgling sound and then it was eerily quiet. I rolled the cylinder of the gun, ejecting the spent cartridges, then replaced them and holstered it. I turned away from the deadly scene and walked back into the house.

"Are you alright? You're not hit?"

"I'm ok. You might want to check outside, although I don't believe it'll do any good. You probably should go ahead and call the undertaker."

He went outside and checked for a pulse on both bodies.

"How you doing, Red? You okay?"

"I am now, although I wish you hadn't killed them on my account."

"If it hadn't been me, it would have been somebody else. They were on the death path long before they ever came to town. I'm just glad they didn't hurt you."

"Thank you, for what you did. I'm grateful." She reached up and placed a kiss on my unshaven face. I turned away. It was too soon for feelings like I was having. I had been a widowed less than a month. It hadn't been long since I had a wife and unborn child. I wasn't ready for these kinds of feelings.

I went back outside. "Get back inside. The Marshall's coming. I'll take care of this. He's a friend of mine. Go on now, back inside."

"Hello Cotton. You have a disagreement with these two fellows?"

"You can see for yourself."

"I suppose these boys are from your past?"

"You supposed right. Sorry for the mess. You know I'm trying to live peaceable the next few years. I really tried to avoid killing'em."

I know that, Cotton. Don't worry about it. You've been a model citizen since you came back here to Crippled Jaw. I'll get some of the boys to clean up this mess."

"I appreciate that, Bart. You're a good friend."

"You have a good night. Tell Denise I was asking about her. See you later."

"I'll do that. Goodnight to you."

With that the Marshall walked back to town.

"What was that all about? I can take care of myself. I'm not afraid to take the blame for killing that scum."

"I know that, Son, but I think it's better if you stay out of sight until you're ready to move on. Those men that killed your wife could still be in the area and they think you're dead, just like your wife. Let them think that until you're ready to brace them. You may have taken those two out in the yard, but they weren't gunmen, unlike the ones that almost killed you. You want to be able to take'em when you meet, don't you?"

"I see what you mean. Does this mean you're going to teach me what I need to know?"

"I reckon you was sent here for a reason. I'd like to do something worthwhile before I'm gone. Yes, I'm going to teach you, but you're going to have to listen and do exactly what I tell you. Can you do that?"

"Sure. If it'll help me to kill those scoundrels. I'll do what you say. No problem."

"I was watching through the window when you went up against those two. You have a natural ability, the vision and reflexes, but you need to hone them, learn how to use these abilities to your advantage. You've been born with a talent that not many processed. However, the most important ability is common sense. And I believe you have that. The second ability is confidence. I believe you have that. Now we need to join all these abilities into one. Being the fastest draw isn't always the best. Hitting the target is probably the one thing you need to learn first."

We did all the practicing about a mile from the house. He would point out things for me to shoot at. At first I didn't hit anything. Every so often he would stop and have a coughing fit.

You want to go back to the house?"

"It won't get no better by going back to the house. Just give me a minute. It'll pass, always does. Doc says not to worry too much until I start coughing up blood, then it's getting worse."

"I wish I could do something for you."

"You just keep getting better. I want to see those men pay for what they done to you. Now, I want you to draw, but don't shoot. Aim first and then pull the trigger slowly. Don't try to be the fastest. Just be the one that hits the target with the first shot."

I drew, took aim and pulled the trigger. Every shot hit the target.

"What happens if someone is faster than that?"

"If he's fast, like you were before, and misses the target, then you'll get him because you took your time and aimed. The more you practice, the faster you'll get. Right now concentrate on hitting the target. The rest will come. I promise."

"Can I ask why you're doing this for me?"

"I wasn't always a gunman. I had a farm just like you. One day when I was out in the fields, some men came by, raped my wife and killed my boy when he tried to help her. He was ten years old. I took my wife to the neighbor's and went hunting for the men. I found them in town at the saloon drinking and bragging about what they had done to that squirt of a kid. I drew my pistol, walked inside and told them to stand up. I shot them as they stood. I don't know if they reached for their guns or not. I just wanted them dead. The sheriff told me later that they each had a gun in their hand when the undertaker came to collect the bodies. I never did go back home. I just couldn't face my wife. I realize now that I was being a fool. It wasn't her fault. I learned later that she was going to have a baby. That really set me off. I couldn't be sure if it was mine or not. I realized later that it had to be mine. I love my daughter more than life itself. I only wish I could have learned what I now know in time, to share it with my wife. I sent money home whenever I could, but it wasn't the same as me being there. I started going from town to town hunting for someone that needed to have someone eliminated. You'd be surprised how many bad people are out there just waiting for someone to come along and do their dirty work for them, and pay for it. I always made sure it was self-defense when I took them out. That's how I got the reputation of being a fast gun."

"That's quite a story. I only want to catch the men who killed my wife. Then I'll quit."

"I want you to promise an old man that that's exactly what you'll do. Don't make the same mistake I did. Revenge needs to end when those men are dead. If not it will consume you and rob you of happiness that you deserve. When it's done. Come back here. I know Denise cares a lot about you. You two could be happy right here on this place."

"I'll do that. When I'm done, I'll come back here."

"Good, let's head back.

CHAPTER FOUR

Each day when we got back home, he would have me soak my arm and hand in a tub of hot salt water. He said it would make my arm stronger, quicker and also take care of that blister on my trigger finger.

"Stay cool and in control. Don't let your temper get you killed. Revenge will get you killed if you go about with a hot head. Study your opponent. Watch him for a day or two, then take what you've learned and confront him. You have the advantage because you know him, but he doesn't know you. Use that knowledge against him and you'll be victorious every time. But if you continue in this line of work for long, there will come a time when you'll not get the chance to study your opponent. You'll have to face him straight up. Then is when a cool head will prevail. Always keep a cool head. No matter the situation. A cool head will prevail."

I was sitting on the front porch looking at the land surrounding Cotton's place and talking to myself.

"This is rich soil, a man should be able to grow anything here. It'd even be good for raising cattle. It'd be the perfect place to settle down with a girl like Denise. Whoa! Where did that come from? I've got no feelings for her, but gratitude for nursing me."

I looked in the mirror at my reflection. The skin was stretched tight over my face bones giving my jaw and chin a skeletal look. My pale blue eyes which were at one time, sharp and shiny were sunken into my face. My dark brown hair was starting to curl at the ends from lack of being cut. My sun bronzed skin was pale and ghostly looking. My shirt was extremely loose fitting, and my pants would have fallen to my knees had I not tightened my belt to the last notch.

Denise had shaved me on many occasions, but now as I looked, my beard had grown and didn't look bad at all.

"I didn't look anything like I did. I don't believe anyone will recognize me. This beard is just what I needed to disguise my looks in case I run across those cretins."

"You ready to go do some more shooting?"

"Sure, I'm ready."

I tightened the cinch, tied my bedroll down, put my left foot in the stirrup and pulled myself into the saddle. I felt a little dizzy, but it passed quickly. I looked toward the house and Denise was watching me. I started to raise my hand in a farewell gesture, but decided against it. I didn't want to say goodbye. I wanted to take her in my arms and smother her with kisses. No! I can't feel this way. It's too soon. I only feel gratitude, that's all. I turned Star away from the house and gave him the go ahead. We left at a gallop behind Cotton. God forgive me, how I wanted to turn in the saddle and see if she is still watching. We rode past the little creek where I would have drowned, if Cotton's friend hadn't come along. I must have crawled from the cabin to the creek, although I don't remember. I stopped in front of the burned out cabin. So many memories, so little time here. I looked around and over under the old oak tree, where Shelly and I had spent many hours making plans for the future, was a mound of dirt. Cotton's friend again. I need to offer him a sincere thank you, but come to think of it, I don't believe I ever saw him until much later.

"You tell Mr. Hunsaker how much I appreciate what he did. And I can't begin to tell you and Denise how much you mean to me." He told me Mr. Hunsaker found me face down in the creek behind my burned cabin. If the bullet hadn't killed me, I would have drowned in that creek. I have no memory before waking in Cotton's home and he was giving me a drink of water. Everything before that is a blank. Of course, there are the dreams. The laughing, taunting faces. And then the fog, the thick fog that blinded me from seeing. The fog, that was like water, dragging me down into its dark depths. And when the fog disappeared for a moment, I could see Shelly trying to hand our unborn baby to me. I tried to reach and then the fog would envelop me.

After a few practice shots.

"I think you're ready. You're as ready as anyone can be. There's nothing left to do except to do it. I don't think you need to come back to the house. It would upset Denise too much to see you go. This way she won't have to watch as you leave."

I reached out my hand for him to shake. He brushed it aside and grabbed me in a bear hug. I didn't tell him I was planning on leaving anyway.

"You take care and remember what you've learned. I don't want to hear about you getting killed in some unforgotten place."

With tears in both our eyes, he mounted up and rode into the setting sun. I watched until he disappeared over the horizon. He had been and was a good friend. I hated to see him go. I hated to leave. However, he had taught me a valuable lesson. How to survive while hunting killers. His name. Cotton Buchanan. The famous legendary Texas gunslinger. I'll always remember that name.

CHAPTER FIVE

I kept practicing even after Cotton said I was good enough. My strength needed to improve and with my strength, my mind needed to be clear and remember what he taught me. I heard later of Cotton's passing. I was in another state when I heard about it. I remembered what he had said when we first met.

"Don't put no store in rumors. It'll get you in trouble. Don't believe in rumors. Never have, never will."

I, also, remembered the promise that I made to him and have since broken many times over. But I guess I didn't break the promise because I still haven't found the men who killed Shelly. I look for them everywhere I travel. I'm sure I'll recognize them. Their faces are burned into my memory. I'm now known as Clint Bowers, the famous gunfighter. I can't count the number of men I've sent to their maker. I collected many bounties. Some say I'm rich, however, there is one thing I'm missing, just like Cotton told me I would. Happiness has eluded me. It's too late for me to return to Denise. Surely by now, she's happily married, and more than likely, has a couple of kids. I can' go back as long as those men are walking this earth. Maybe I'll find them in the next town.

I pulled on the reins of Star, stopping on the edge of this town, so like the many towns I've passed through. I looked around surveying the surroundings. I did this with every town. Teachings from Cotton Buchanan that I won't forget. I gave Star a nudge and we started down the street. We pulled up in front of the local watering hole. Don't recall the name. Doesn't matter. It was like all the others. I had just stepped down from the saddle when I heard my name.

"Bowers! Clint Bowers?"

I turned and faced the sound. He was young, maybe seventeen or eighteen years old. Not old enough to die. He didn't look like he was shaving yet, needed a haircut under a floppy felt hat pulled low on his forehead. He was dressed in farmer's clothes except for his gun. The holster was still shiny and new looking. He had it tied down on his leg. The pistol, what I could see of it was a pearl handled revolver. It, also, looked new and unused. He was standing about twenty feet away. If he got a shot off, he could hit me. Which meant I had to get him first, even with letting him draw first.

"You don't have to do this, Kid."

He made his move, but he was as slow as molasses. His gun was just clearing his holster, when he was knocked backwards onto the dusty street from the force of the slug, as it entered the center of his chest. His feet twitched a couple of times and then he was still.

The sheriff came rushing around the corner with his gun drawn.

"Hold it right there, Bowers. I've got you covered. Holster your weapon."

"I could drop you before you could pull the trigger, but I won't. It was self-defense. Ask anybody."

"I'll do that, as soon as you holster that hog leg." I pushed my .45 back into the holster and stood beside my horse.

"He's right, Sheriff. The young one challenged him. He was faster, that's the way it happened." The others nodded, confirming it was true.

"Alright. I reckon you're telling it true. But I want you out of town in two hours. Understand?"

"I hear and obey. I'll leave when I'm ready which will probably be in about two hours."

"Don't push me, Bowers. You may be fast but that don't keep me from doing my job."

"I'll be leaving as you requested. Ok?" I walked into the saloon. Looked at every face, turned around and walked back out. I walked the boardwalk down one side and up the other. I stopped in the sheriff's office.

"Mind if I take a gander at your posters?"

"Help yourself, if it'll make you leave town any faster."

"I'm not the enemy here? You realize that, don't you?"

"I just know trouble follows you whenever you go. That's something I don't need in my town."

"I'll leave as soon as I finish looking at these. Can I take this one? I could make use of three thousand dollars."

"Can't we all? Take whatever you want and say goodbye."

"Goodbye Sheriff." I folded the poster, put in my shirt pocket, tipped my hat to him and left. I placed my left foot in the stirrup and pulled myself into the saddle. I gave Star his head, we turned west and rode out of town. I don't remember the name of that town. I just remember a seventeen year old kid, and the look on his face, when my bullet knocked him down. Sometimes, when I close my eyes, I see many such faces along with the killers of Shelly. If I could only find them and settle the score with them, then I could quit. It was just another town, another life forced out into eternity by my hand.

I get tired of traveling from town to town trying to outrun my reputation. Not only do I collect bounties, but I have to face every hothead that wants to build his reputation by eliminating me. I'm still alive, thanks to Cotton Buchanan.

CHAPTER SIX

I've remembered everything Cotton taught me. I've kept that teaching except for the one time. That's when my hot headedness cost me an eye and almost claimed my life. However, I did kill the man before I lost consciousness. That's the only reason I lived that day. He couldn't follow through with a second shot, because he died that day. I'm reminded every day when I try to look to my left. I try very hard not to repeat that mistake. I also met someone that day that caused me to change my life.

I rode into this small town as usual. I had just gotten off my horse when this young punk called me out.

"You called Bowers? The Gunfighter/Bounty Hunter?"

"What if I am? Who's asking?"

"My name's Kid Rovello. Everybody's gonna know my name after today. I'm gonna kill you today. Get ready to die."

"I've got no quarrel with you. Why don't you walk away and you'll live to see tomorrow's sunrise?"

"I understand you got into this business because of what some lowlifes did to your wife. If I'd been there she would have had more fun than she did with them."

I could feel the anger boil up inside me. I thought the top of my head was going to explode. My eyes blurred for a second.

I felt something tug at my hat and saw it laying in the dirt. I, also, felt something warm sliding down the side of my head. I drew and fired, but in my haste the shot went wild. His second shot hit me on the side of my head right where I felt the liquid running down. I could feel the blackness closing in on me. I fired this time from pure instinct. I saw him crumple to the ground before I lost consciousness.

CHAPTER SEVEN

Old memories flooded my head.

"Cotton? Denise? Are you there?"

"Don't talk now. Just rest. You'll understand in time where you are. No. Don't touch your eye. It's covered with a bandage. We won't know about it until the bandage is removed. You just take it easy and rest."

The darkness closed in again. I saw the faces of Shelly's killers. This time I saw each lifeless face staring up at nothing. Each one had a bullet hole in his forehead. My bullet. I saw Cotton showing me how to draw and shoot. Denise was there telling me to shave my beard. They were all there except Shelly. Where was Shelly? Where was my wife?

"It's ok. You can open your eye. I know it's gonna be hard at first, but you'll grow used to it. Now, take a sip of this?"

He lifted my head. It felt as if it was exploding. I took a sip and tried to swallow. It felt like a lump in my throat.

"Try again. Your throat is dry from just lying here."

I took a small swig and it felt good. I took another.

"Whoa there. Not too much. Just a little is best for you. You lay back and rest. I'll give you more a little later."

I put my hand up and felt my face. The left side was covered with a bandage. Was I going to be able to see with this eye? I can't continue with what I do if I can't see. I closed my eye and let the darkness claim me once again.

I woke the next morning hearing birds singing outside the window.

"Good. You're awake. How would you like to try to eat something?"

Here stood an elderly gray headed man with a square face and a large protruding Adam's apple. He was dressed in black trousers and a rumpled white shirt with the sleeves rolled up. He was old and stick thin.

"Sounds good to me. Maybe if I get something in my belly, this headache will ease up?'

"I'm afraid that headache will be with you for a couple more days. The doctor says you just need to take it easy. Don't exert yourself and in a couple days it should be gone."

"The doctor was here?"

"Yes. He's been here many times."

"How long have I been here? Is my horse alright? Did someone take him to the livery stable?"

"Let's see. I guess it's going on eight days. Yes. A little over a week. And yes, your horse has been well taken care of. He's in the barn behind the house. You get better and you can go see him. Can you sit up and take a little of this soup? You need my help?"

"I think I can manage."

I sat up and leaned against the wall. He handed me a bowl with a spoon.

"Um. This is good. Did you make it?"

"Oh no. One of my parishioners made it. A young widow woman. She's a very good cook. I hardly do any cooking. My people take good care of me."

"You a preacher? I'm in a preacher's house, in a preacher's bed. Hold on to your hats. The roofs going to crash down on us."

"I assure you the roof's not going to crash down on us."

"You say your folks cook for you. That means you're alone?"

"Yes. I'm sad to say my wife passed almost one year ago. Was married to her nigh on fifty years."

"Maybe you and the widow woman can work something out?"

"I'm much too old to be looking for another wife. I'm content just preaching God's Word to these blessed people. Do you want some more soup? I think there's enough for half a bowl."

"Did you give me your soup?"

"I had a big dinner. You need it more than I."

"I'll not eat another bite. You eat what is left. I need to lay back down anyway. My head is starting to spin."

"I'll check in on you a little later."

I didn't hear anything until the next morning. That pesky bird was outside the window making a heck of a noise. I sat up in bed and noticed my head was feeling better. I again felt the bandage on the left side of my face. It felt huge.

Maybe I can get out of bed if I take it easy. I threw the covers back, swung my legs over the side and pushed with my arms. I was standing. My head wasn't spinning. I didn't feel dizzy. I put one foot out in front of me, then another and another. I had almost reached the door when it opened. A young man carrying a satchel walked in.

"That's quite an accomplishment. I didn't expect you to be walking for at least a couple more days, maybe more. I'm Doctor Morgan and you are?"

"Names Clint Bowers. Maybe you've heard of me?"

"Yes, I've heard the name. If there were less people like you, the undertaker would go out of business. How are you feeling?"

"I've been better. When can I take this bandage off?"

"How about now. I need to take a look at that eye. Sit here in this chair."

I sat and he took some small scissors and began unraveling the bandage from around my head.

"Close your right eye. Let me know if you see any light in this eye?"

I could feel the bandage as he unwrapped it from around my head. I couldn't see anything.

"Anything yet? I've almost got them all off. Any light at all?

"Nothing. It's dark as dark as the darkest cave. No light at all."

"I was afraid of that. I'm afraid that bullet crushed a nerve in this eye. I had hoped when I first examined you that the outcome would be different. I'm sorry I couldn't do more."

"It's not your fault. I don't even blame the man who shot me. I place the blame squarely where it belongs. With me. Everything happens for a reason. I just have to figure out the reason for this setback. Thank you for trying Doc."

"What's the verdict, Doc? Is he going to be able to see with that eye?"

"I'm afraid not. He will never see with that eye again."

"Kind of handicaps my work, don't it?"

"Perhaps you can find another line of work. The Lord may have plans for you that you don't fully realize yet."

"I think the Lord forgot about me many years ago. I know I quit talking to Him back when Shelly died. Shelly was my wife."

"You may have quit on Him, but He didn't quit on you. God doesn't ever quit on one of His children. You are one of His children, aren't you?"

"I was at one time. At least I thought I was and then they killed Shelly. That's when I felt like He deserted both of us."

"Maybe He had something for Shelly to do in Heaven. That's why he called her home. God doesn't make mistakes. He doesn't desert His children. They do, however, desert Him, but they usually come back. Are you ready to come back to Him? I overheard you telling the doc that everything happens for a reason. Maybe this is God's way of telling you it's time to come back to Him?"

"But I've killed so many men and I've still got to find Shelly's killers. I can't rest until they're all dead and in the ground."

"What if you never find them? Are you going to continue on this path of destruction? You've lived this time because God let you live.

"For what purpose?"

"I can't tell you, but I think you know what you have to do."

"Do you think He'll take me back?"

"Of course, all you have to do is ask."

I bowed my head right there in front of the doc and the preacher and asked God to forgive me my sins and let me be one of His children again. I felt a peace that I hadn't felt in years flow into my heart. A sweet calmness came over me.

"Does this mean if I see Shelly's killers, I have to walk away?"

"I think you already know the answer to that. You will do what needs to be done should the occasion arise."

"I think you should get back in bed for now. Get a good night's rest and we'll tackle a new day tomorrow. How's that sound to you?"

"Sounds like a plan. How can I ever repay either of you?"

"As for me, this is what I do."

"The same goes for me. I only wish it hadn't cost an eye for you to see clearly."

"Thank you both. I mean that with all my heart."

They both left the room. My mind was racing, it seemed like ninety miles an hour. So many thoughts. If I could no longer be a bounty hunter or a gunfighter, then would I be able to serve God in a way that He would want me to?

"Lord, please let me know what you want me to do with my life. Amen."

I woke the next morning to the sound of that pesky bird. At least this morning it was singing a cheerful song. At least it sounded cheerful. I reached and strapped on my gun-belt from force of habit, I suppose. After all, I could wear a gun and not be a gunfighter. Most everyone carried a gun for protection. I might come up on a rattlesnake. I would need a gun for that.

"Good morning, Clint. How you feeling this morning? I scrambled a few eggs and fried some bacon, if you think you can stomach an old man's cooking."

"I'm sure I'll survive. Do you have any coffee?"

"Some of the best coffee in three counties. That's one thing I do very well. You want black or sugar and cream?"

"Black, the blacker the better. I think I know what God wants me to do. I'm gonna be a preacher. Like you."

"I'm sure you'll make a fine preacher, but you don't want to be like me. You'll be Clint Bower the preacher just like you were Clint Bower the gunfighter. I think each man should be himself. That's the thing that will cause people to listen. Tell your story of where you started and where you are now. Folks will listen if you tell it with love."

"I realize I owe you so much already, but will you do me the honor of teaching me what I need to know."

"It would be my honor to send one of God's preachers on the path to teach others about His wonderful love. Here's your coffee. Now tell me is that great coffee?"

I didn't want to hurt his feelings, but I couldn't lie to him.

"I'm very sorry, but this is probably the worst coffee, I've ever tasted."

"You're starting off on the right path. Being truthful. I agree, this is bad stuff. Let's hope the bacon and eggs are better."

They were better. A lot better. We settled down to business right after breakfast. He told me how to put the words, together so folks could grasp what I was trying to get across to them.

"Above everything else, always be truthful. That's what people want. A preacher that will tell the truth."

What about my firearm? When I'm preaching, should I wear it?"

"I really can't advise you about that. What you need to do is talk to God about it and I know He will give you peace about the matter. Always remember, He's waiting to hear from you at all times. He's the one to lean on."

He read to me from a tattered old Bible, many stories. I suppose my heart had been so empty it soaked it all in like a dry dish towel. Then he handed it to me and let me read. I just couldn't get enough. I had lost the sight in my eye, but I could see clearer now than I had in my entire life.

I promised the preacher and I promised God that I would tell His story and mine to any and all who would listen. I wanted others to share with me how wonderful it can be, if we only turn to Jesus.

You realize not everyone will want to hear this wonderful message. Some will even challenge you with a gun. Some will remember you from days gone by and want to build their reputation by killing you. You asked the other day about wearing your gun. I think after much thought and prayer about this matter, as much as you might want to, you can't lay your gun aside. It has to be carried side by side with the Bible every day. Maybe someday, you'll be able to travel without your weapon, but not yet. I want you to have this Bible. It has been with me ever since I began my ministry too many years ago."

"I can't take your Bible. You're going to need it."

"Clint, I've been doing this long enough, if I can't remember the Bible verses that I need, then I probably should quit. No. You take it. It has served me well. I hope it will do the same for you. Now let's go to the store and dress you like a preacher."

When we came out of the store, I was dressed all in black from the top to the bottom. Black trousers, black shirt, black hat, black boots, even a black string tie and a black frock coat. I even bought a black holster and belt and traded my pearl handled Colt.45, single action, for a black handled Colt.45, double action. I was looking like a preacher, but somehow I wasn't feeling like one. My new clothes were so dark, that if the sun hid behind a cloud, you wouldn't be able to see me.

"Don't worry. You'll get used to them just like you're getting used to only having one eye. You'll feel better after a few sermons under your belt."

"I don't think I can pull this off. I'm a gunfighter, not a preacher."

"Don't tell me. Tell God."

With those words, he took off walking back to his house. I reluctantly followed behind, looking very conspicuously in my new outfit. Maybe he was right. After a few days it would feel right.

"I think you're ready to strike out on your own. There's a little town east of here that doesn't have a preacher. The folks will be ripe to hear the kind of message that you have to share. How about it? You ready?"

"Is it alright to be scared? 'Cause that's what I'm feeling. I never felt this scared when I was facing a fast gun."

"It will get easier the more you do it. Now mount up and leave, before you bring an old man to tears. It's been a pleasure knowing you and calling you friend. Goodbye and God bless you."

"Preacher. You know I don't know your name. I always just called you Preacher."

"I've been called Preacher for so long I've begun to think that's my name. However, my mother named me Joshua Elias. Forney is the last name, but you can just call me Preacher because that's what I am. Always have been, always will be until I pass from this mortal world. Again, I bid you farewell. May God richly bless you my son. Now skedaddle." As he slapped my horse and I was off to begin my new job.

CHAPTER EIGHT

I arrived in a little settlement called Silver Bluff at dawn. After riding all night, I was exhausted. All I wanted to do was find a place to crash and sleep forever. I rode up to the livery stable. A man stepped out from the door. A big burly man with bib overalls, a floppy hat. He spit a stream of tobacco juice across the yard.

"Howdy stranger. Name's Lars Kincaid. Reckon you need to board your horse? Say you look like a preacher. Ain't seen nobody like you in a month of Sundays? You figure on saying some words here in Silver Bluff, do you?"

"I might have something to say after I've rested a bit. Mind if I settle in with my horse?"

"Shore thing, but why don't you go to Lulu's Boarding House down at the end of the street. That's where the other preacher's always stayed, although like I said it's been a while. I'm pretty sure she'll find a bed for you. You being a preacher and all. Go ahead. I'll take care of your horse, no charge, you being a preacher and all."

"Thank you kind sir, I'll remember you in my prayers."

"That's all I could expect, you being a..."

"I know, me being a preacher and all. Goodnight to you."

"And goodnight to you."

I walked down the street which was deserted this time of morning, except for the shopkeepers that were opening for business. Some of them stopped what they were doing and nodded to me as I passed. I reached my destination, noticed a pretty newly whitewashed building with fancy curtains on the windows. I opened the little gate and walked up to the door. I raised my hand to knock when the door opened.

"Oh my! You scared me. I wasn't expecting anyone to be standing in the door." She was wearing a blue flowered cotton dress, covered by a dark blue apron. On the pudgy side, her nervousness showed, as she twisted a dish towel in her hands that were dusted with flour.

"Say, you're not a preacher are you?"

"I sure hope I am. My benefactor told me this is the finest fashion for preachers."

"That's funny. I hope you have a sense of humor in the pulpit. Why are you wearing a gun? All the preachers I've ever seen wasn't wearing no gun. You sure you're a preacher?"

"We'll find out Sunday morning. I was wondering if I could get a bed for a couple hours."

"Why sure you can. After all, this is a boarding house. You get a room for free, you being a preacher and all. Follow me. You got a bag or something?"

"I'm so tired I completely forgot about them. I left them at the livery stable."

"Not to worry, come on. We'll get you settled in and I'll send my boy to get your things. Come along."

"Thank you, ma'am. You're very kind."

"Ain't nothing too good for you, you being a preacher and all. Here's your room. There's water in the pitcher. A clean towel hanging there. Anything else you need can wait till you wake up. Goodnight to you, Preacher." Saying that she closed the door. I collapsed onto the bed, not bothering to even remove my gun belt. I was out cold in no time.

I awoke the next morning when the sun started shining across my face. I washed my face, ran my fingers through my hair and went downstairs.

"Good morning, Preacher. I trust you got some rest?"

"Thank you, ma'am, I did."

"Do you want to take your meals here or at the cafe? You'd be better off eating here, 'cause there'd be no charge, you being a preacher and all."

"If it's not too much trouble, I would count it an honor to dine with a beautiful woman, such as yourself."

"You do have a way with words, don't you? Wouldn't expect no less from a preacher. I have to fix for the other boarders, so one more don't take no extra work."

"Thank you, ma'am."

"Call me Lulu. Most everybody does."

"All right, Lulu. You can call me Clint."

"I couldn't do that. You being a Preacher and all. I'll call you Reverend or Preacher. Wouldn't be right calling the preacher by his first name."

Miss Lulu was a very good cook. Her meatloaf was some of the best I've ever tasted. There were five other men staying in the house. All different sizes and shapes. Different occupations. Two were salesmen with Silver Bluff serving as home base. One worked as a clerk in the general store. One worked in the bank. The last man with the thick spectacles, worked in the post office. They seemed to get along together. After meals, some went outside for a cigar. Others sat in the parlor reading or playing checkers. I wasn't asked to join any of them. It was like I had a disease and they were afraid of catching it. I would either walk around town or go to my room and read my Bible. Miss Lulu was very friendly. Most of the town people that I ran into were friendly, but not overly so. My work was cut out for me in this small country town. I guess my predecessor spooked them into believing that all men dressed in black and carrying a Bible were all crooked. Somehow, I had to change their believing that way. I figured it was time to visit the church house. Mrs. Brown pointed me in the right direction. It was located about five hundred yards south of town on a little knoll. I stopped a few yards short of the door. I shook my head in disbelief. How could God's people let His building get so rundown? The tall grass made it a chore to navigate my way to the door. The building was badly in need of a paint job. That was only the beginning. The front door was hanging on one hinge. I pulled it open and went inside. There were only six pews, with three of them turned upside down. Leaves, small limbs and dirt covered the floor, which I noticed had some loose boards. I looked up and saw blue sky in several places. I walked forward. The homemade wooden pulpit was knocked off the platform and laying on its side. The only positive thing I saw was a six foot, hand carved, cross hanging on the wall behind the pulpit. As I stood on the platform looking out over the pews, I imagined them filled with believers. The small room had two stained glass windows on each side. It seemed a miracle they were still intact. I dropped to my knees, looked up through the holes in the roof,

"Lord. It seems You gave me a big job here. You know I can't do this alone. Give me the wisdom and the words to convince Your children of their responsibility for this house of worship. I know You don't make mistakes and I would ask for Your guidance that I don't either. Amen."

I picked myself off the floor, brushed off my pants.

"Excuse me, Preacher. My name's Solomon Black. I'm the town's carpenter."

Mr. Black was a large man. I could tell he worked outside because of his suntanned face and his large hands covered with calluses.

"I noticed you coming up the trail to the church. I want to offer my services to help repair the church house. I haven't had any work in nigh on two months. I would be willing to work at half wages. I wouldn't ask for nothing, 'cepten, my family's mighty hungry. If you want to know about my work, I carved the cross behind the pulpit."

"Here's a few dollars to tide you over until other arrangements can be made."

"I can't take a Preacher's money. It's supposed to be the other way around."

"I'm here to help God's children in any way I can. If that means letting you have a few dollars, then that's what I'll do. Please take it. We'll call it a loan."

"Well, if it's a loan until I can get back on my feet. I accept. Thank you, Preacher. May God bless you and yours?"

"It's only me. But I thank you for the kind words. Who do I need to talk to about donating money so wc can get started?"

"Mr. Levi Johansen. He owns a big cattle ranch about ten miles south of town. He's the money man around here. But he's not real friendly, especially to Preachers. Tread carefully when you go see him"

That's the same name I heard from Mrs. Brown.

"Thank you kindly, Solomon Black. I'll talk to you later." I watched him leave walking a little straighter with a few dollars in his pocket. I took another look around and shook my head. If I swept the floor and straightened up the furniture, we could hold services here, if it didn't rain. In the meantime, I need to get busy convincing folks I'm not a monster. I'm just another soul struggling in this old world amongst them. Where to start, that's the question? Start with the ones who will talk to you was the answer I received. I went to the livery stable to pick up Star.

CHAPTER NINE

"What can you tell me about Levi Johansen?"

"Levi Johansen owns the biggest cattle ranch in the county. If you want to get the town folks interested in repairing the church building, you have to get him to encourage them, by being the first one to donate." This part of the ministry was one part I didn't care for. I felt like I was forcing them to give their money to God when they should be happy and willing to give because of the blessings they received from God. I mounted Star and headed southeast. The Ranch was located about ten to eleven miles out of town. Not only did the small valleys have grass and water, it was also rugged country. Where the land started to rise, it wasn't all grass and open sky. It was ravines, rocky outcroppings and a few trees thrown in. It didn't look like good country for raising cattle, but there in front of me was a sign hanging from two long poles in the ground. Circle J Ranch. I guess that showed how much I knew about raising cows. The trail past the gate was Sandy Loam. Now that's a good soil for a garden. We had that on our place. Shelley and me. We had a big garden on the east side of the cabin. We got some very good vegetables out of that garden. The cellar was almost full when it all came crashing down.

The sky was clear blue with a hot yellow sun beating down on me.

"It's sure a hot one, huh Star?" Star shook his head as if he understood what I said. I mopped my brow with my bandana and put my hat back on my head. Star was in a hurry it seemed. I guess he smelled water. It was a short distance to the main house. A big two story house. The kind of house that a very prosperous rancher would have. It had red tile shingles on the roof. A big high Adobe fence surrounded it. A large covered porch went all the way across the front. Off to the side a good hundred yards or so was a big barn, a corral and a bunkhouse. There were four good looking horses in the large corral. A cowboy was working one of them in a second smaller corral. I rode Star over to the water trough and let him bend his head into the water. It looked so refreshing that I climbed out of the saddle and dunked my head in the cool liquid.

A man rode up on a beautiful black stallion. He was dressed in typical cowboy garb. The only thing I noticed different about him was he was clean. His round face was clean shaven. What hair I could see below his Stetson hat was turning Gray. I wiped my face and stood up straight. His voice spoke with authority that demanded respect.

"What'd you want here, stranger?"

"My name's Clint Bower. I'm the new preacher and I'd like to talk to Mr. Johansen, if he's available?"

"What's your business with him? He's a very busy man. If it's money you're after, he ain't interested."

"I'd like to hear that from him, if you don't mind?"

"You're hearing it from him. I'm Levi Johansen. Now I suggest you mount up and ride out of here. Every preacher I ever met was as dishonest as the day is long. Now mount and ride."

"I didn't ride ten miles just to be turned away without you hearing what I have to say."

"You talk kinda tough for a preacher."

"I can be tough if I need to be. Like I said, I'll leave when you've heard me speak my piece. Not before."

"Ok. I'm listening."

"I came here because I need your help and I don't ask for help lightly, and then not from many people. It seems the town watches what you do. If you were to make a sizeable donation to help repair the church building, then they would fall in line, do the right thing and do their part. But they're waiting to see what you'll do."

"Why do I want to give money for something that's not going to last. The last preacher took what money that was collected and left the county. What makes you any different than him?"

"If we could sit down with a cool drink, I believe I can convince you I am different. Give me fifteen minutes, then I'll leave, empty handed, if that's what you want."

"Come on inside. I think there's some lemonade, unless you want something stronger?"

"Lemonade sounds great. Lead the way. Will my horse be alright here?"

"Hey Slugger! Take care of the preacher's horse. Follow me."

I followed him into that big house. How in earth could a man justify living like this when so many others were living in shacks? The inside was even more fancy and spacious than the outside. He led me into a large room with a fireplace across one end. There were pictures hanging on every wall. A large Longhorn Steer's horns adorned the wall above the mantle.

"Grab a seat. I'll be right back with the drinks." He returned shortly with two very tall, very full glasses filled with lemonade.

"Thank you. It looks delicious." I took a long swallow and smacked my lips. "It tastes as good as it looks."

"Let's hear your spiel. It better be good."

I began at the beginning. How the renegades killed Shelley and ended with me riding out here to see him.

"Ok. That's a real good story, but why should I get involved?"

"Because of who you are. Or better yet, who you used to be. I did some asking around town, about you, before I made the trip out here. It seems at one time you accepted Christ as your Savior. You were one of the biggest contributors in the county. The church building wouldn't have gotten built if you hadn't stepped in and got it going. I think you've let this ranch and this fancy house with all these material things cloud your judgment. I believe you've quit on God. I here to tell you that He hasn't quit on you. He's waiting, in fact, He's been waiting for quite a while. Do you remember how happy and content you were when you were serving Him. You can have that joy and peace again. All you have to do, well, I believe you know what you have to do."

"Yes. I know what to do. Would you pray with me, Preacher?"

"Of course I will." We prayed together right there in the fancy room of that fancy house.

A soul came back home that day. This is what it's like to be a preacher. Helping a lost sheep find his way back to the flock. I left Levi Johansen, that day, with a promise from him that he would come to church on Sunday, stand in front of the people and proclaim his new found faith. The church building was going to be repaired. We might even get a steeple for it. The ride back didn't seem as far as it did going.

"Thank You, Father, for using me today. Please continue to use me in a way that will bring glory and honor to Thy name. Amen."

CHAPTER TEN

I had just finished my first sermon in our newly renovated building. The pews were filled and we had been talking about enlarging the auditorium. Quite a difference from the very first words I spoke in this little building. There were only two families and Levi Johansen on the day. It didn't rain for which I was thankful. Mr. Johansen did what he said he would. He stood in front of that little group and proclaimed his newfound faith. He challenged each person present to do the same and to invite them to the next service. It took some getting used to for the folks to see my pistol lying beside the open Bible, however, in time they accepted it after hearing my story of how I arrived in their town.

Today I had shook everyone's hand, wished them well and watched them go their separate ways. I was walking back to the boarding house when I saw a vaguely familiar face. My mind kicked into memory mode. I searched for whom that face belonged to. Then it hit me square in the heart. He was the young leader of the group that killed Shelly many years ago.

I can't begin to count how many men I've sent to meet their maker while I searched for Shelly's killers. I can say they were all classified as self-defense. Of course, sometimes I would have to force them to draw against me. I did this by insulting, calling them names. Anything to make them lose control. Then it was just a matter of pulling the trigger. I collected a lot of money on most of them. I was always searching for the killers. I searched every saloon, every watering hole in every town and settlement. It's like they disappeared from the face of the earth. I kept assuring myself that surely they haven't been killed by someone else. That wouldn't be fair. It was my responsibility and one that I took very seriously at one time. I'm not so sure now. I've been happy being a Preacher. Helping the lost find their way. But now I have what I've been wanting, almost my entire life, right here in front of me. It's been nice not having to always be looking over your shoulder and looking forward at the same time. Now the opportunity to fulfill my vow is here.

I walked over to him as he was getting off his horse.

"Hello Preacher. If you're looking for someone to save, you got the wrong man."

"You don't remember me, don't you?"

"Should I? I don't travel the same road as a Preacher. So no, I don't remember you."

"I've been searching for you and your partners for years. And here you are delivered to me just like a thanksgiving turkey."

"I don't know you. I ain't never seen you before."

"Do you remember a young couple on a farm about fourteen years ago? You and your partners had your way with the woman, then shot her. Then you turned your gun on me and shot me in the chest. Here's the scar to prove it."

As I ripped open my shirt to reveal where the bullet had been removed.

"You can't shoot me. You're a preacher."

"I haven't always been a preacher and I have unfinished business with you from before I became a preacher."

"You orta be dead. How come you're alive?"

"I had a good friend come along and nursed me back to health. He, also, taught me a few things about how to use a gun. Maybe you've heard of him? Cotton Buchanan?"

"Buchanan's been dead for years. Got himself killed in Laredo. I heard about it when it happened."

"You shouldn't put too much stock in rumors. They are greatly exaggerated. Now, I'm going to put one of those lessons to use. I'm not going to kill you, but I want you to walk over to the sheriff's office and turn yourself in. But before you do that, I want you to tell me where to find your partners."

"I ain't gonna tell you nothing. Besides it won't do you no good when you're dead."

"As you wish. Remember, I gave you the chance to live. Anytime you're ready."

I stood with my hand hovering over my pistol. Sweat trickled down his face, into his eyes. He blinked, trying to remove it. His hand twitched and he went for his gun.

My slug entered his chest just to the right of the center. The exact same place he had shot me years ago. He staggered the death dance before the momentum of his body threw him to the dusty street. His pistol half way out of his holster. The crimson blood started pooling under his body. I walked over to where he lay.

"I forgive you for killing my wife." I looked up to the sky.

"Lord, You know I took no pleasure in killing that scum. I gave him the opportunity to turn himself in. I ask forgiveness for taking another man's life. Amen."

The sheriff came rushing up.

"What happened here, Preacher?"

"This man murdered a young woman years ago. I asked him nicely to go see you about it. He refused. It's that simple."

"Any of you folks witness this shooting?"

"It's like the Preacher said. He told the man to turn himself in to you and the man went for his gun. I ain't never seen nobody draw that fast. It was like a rattlesnake striking. Lightning fast."

"Somebody go get the undertaker. Preacher, you come over to the office and I'll take your statement."

CHAPTER ELEVEN

In the four years I was in Silver Bluff, I had two more incidents that I couldn't avoid. One was a man from my past, although he didn't know that until he saw me. He was about the same age as me. His name was Link Baxter. He wore two holsters tied down and was known far and wide as a fast gun. He came into Silver Bluff riding a brown Sorel mare. He dismounted in front of the saloon.

"I hear you folks are hiding a fast gun here? I understand he calls himself a man of the cloth. A Preacher of sorts. How can a Preacher be fast with a gun? Why don't you tell him Link Baxter is here to see him? He'll know what I want."

They came to the church where Solomon Black and me were doing some patch work on the wall.

"Man in town wants to see you, Preacher. Says his name is Link Baxter Said you'd know what he wants."

"Yes, I know what he wants. Where is he?"

"Last I saw he was in front of the saloon."

"Thanks for telling me."

"Is there going to be trouble, Preacher?"

"I'm afraid so, Mr. Black. You keep working. I'll return shortly." I picked up my holster that I had removed while working, strapped it around my waist. I nodded at Mr. Black and walked away from the church building. I walked down Main Street and turned onto Orchard Street. There he was standing next to his horse. I stopped about ten yards away.

"Ah. Here you are. Come closer. Let's make this interesting."

"We don't have to do this, Link. We're getting too old for this."

"As long as I'm still breathing, I'm not too old. Say, don't I know you? It's been a long time, but I remember when you lost that eye down in Bufford. So this is where you been hiding. I always wondered where you disappeared to. Well, it don't matter none, we're here now."

"I really wish you wouldn't do this. It's unnecessary."

"Not for me. This is what I do. I've killed twenty two men. You're gonna be twenty three. I have to be number one."

He started walking toward me. He stopped when he was fifteen feet away.

"I never did hear your name back there in Bufford. I need to know the name of the person I kill, so I can put it on his tombstone."

"My name isn't important."

"Have it your way. Anytime you're ready, Preacher."

He was fast, extremely fast, but just not fast enough. He looked down at the crimson red that was beginning to stain his shirt. He struggled to stay on his feet. He looked from his shirt to me.

"You can't beat me. I'm Link Baxter, fastest gun alive. This is a mistake. I can't be killed by no Preacher." With those last words, his legs no longer able to support him, he crumpled to the ground. He still had his two guns in his hands, one with ten notches. The other with eleven. There would be no more notches carved in those handles. Not today. Nor any other day.

CHAPTER TWELVE

The church building has had two additions since I came here. It was a good feeling knowing that God was using me. We had four Deacons, with Levi Johansen being the head Deacon. He, also, led the singing with his new lady friend playing the piano. She had just moved from Philadelphia and opened a dress shop. The piano had been donated by The Watering Hole Saloon, on Orchard Street. The owner and his oldest son were just baptized last month.

"I have been praying for Sam to be saved ever since we were married. It's because of you that he finally did it. Thank you so much, Preacher."

"Thank God, Mrs. Flannigan, He's the one does the saving and adding names to the Book."

"I'll see you and the boys back at the wagon, Gertrude. I need to talk to the Preacher for a minute."

"Alright dear, come along boys. We'll wait for Papa in the wagon."

Preacher, what am I to do about owning and running a saloon?"

"Sam. I don't think you have anything to worry yourself about. I figure men are going to drink no matter who runs it. It gives you and your family a decent living, doesn't it?"

"It does that alright."

"Just use the wisdom and common sense that God gave you and I think everything will be ok."

"Thank you, Preacher, you're a real blessing to this town."

"Thank you, Sam. See you next Sunday, if not before."

I had been in Silver Bluff for four years. They were happy years. I grew to love the people and I would like to think they thought highly of me. There was a young man that reminded me of myself at his age. He claimed God had called him to be a Preacher. Who was I to question his calling? He spent a year studying at the seminary back east. He worked beside me for a year. I felt at the end of that year, he was ready to have a ministry of his own. I spent many hours praying on it.

Finally, I received an answer. It was time for me to move on and let this young man take my church. The congregation wasn't happy about me leaving, although they had no problem with Levi Junior stepping into my shoes. Yes, the young man was the son of Levi Johansen. He was the perfect choice for the new Pastor of Silver Bluff Baptist Church.

The congregation held a big going away party for me. There were more than just church members at that celebration. So many people attended that it had to be moved from the church to the town square.

I had been there four years and was just now getting to meet some of the citizens. They claimed they had been planning to attend services, but something always came up to prevent them from doing so. The day ended with many handshakes all around and I must admit, a few tears were shed that day.

The day ended on a melancholy note. I had my things packed. Star was saddled and raring to go. I pulled myself up into the saddle and with a wave of my hand and a nod of my head, we rode out and away from Silver Bluff, Texas. It was a sad day, yet I felt an exciting feeling for the path ahead. I had faith that God would have a place prepared for this Preacher.

CHAPTER THIRTEEN

God hadn't given any specific place to go, so I just pointed Star into the setting sun and rode on. Sometime after the sun had hidden behind the horizon, I set up camp in a little draw with a natural spring close by. I removed the saddle from Star and led him to the water. He put his head down and began slurping up the cool liquid. When he was finished, I hobbled him in a patch of green grass just off the bank of the stream. I gathered some wood and built a small fire. I made a pot of coffee and heated a can of beans. While that was cooking I spread out my bedroll, using my saddle as a pillow. It didn't look very good. I guess I was spoiled from sleeping in a nice soft bed in Miss Brown's Boarding House. I wrapped my bandanna around my hand and poured myself a cup of coffee.

"Thank You Lord for a good cup of black coffee. Now, if You could give me a hint as to where You want me to go. It would be greatly appreciated. Amen."

I ate half the beans and drank two more cups of coffee. I set the skillet aside along with the coffee pot, to the side of the fire, which had started to die down. I removed my boots, my gun-belt and stretched out on my hard bed.

It was a restless night for me. Some of the old nightmares returned. I hadn't seen those images for quite some time. Maybe it was being on the road again that caused them to return.

I added some wood to the fire and got it going again. I shook the coffee pot and there was still some in it, so I sliced a few slices of bacon to the leftover beans.

I sure was missing Mrs. Brown's cooking. I need to stop dwelling on the past and focus on the future. Think about what I'm going to do in the next town I come to.

I had just finished the beans and bacon and was drinking the last cup of coffee when.

"Hello! The camp! Ok to ride in?"

"Ride on in." I reached for my pistol and held it so it couldn't be seen.

"Didn't expect to see anybody this far from town. What you doing here by yourself? Me and my two brothers don't never go no place alone. There's some mean fellers out here."

They were a scraggy threesome. It had been a while since they had water on the outside. The one doing the talking climbed off his horse. The other two stayed mounted.

"You got any extra grub? We ain't had nothing to eat since day before yesterday. That shore smells good."

"Why don't you tell your brothers to climb off their horses and I'll fry up some bacon and beans?"

"I don't need to tell'em. They kin hear ok. You boys git off your animals. This gentlemen is gonna fix us some breakfast. Ain't that nice of him?"

"I would ask one favor of you boys."

"What's that?"

"I'd ask you to stand on my right side. I get nervous when I can't see everyone. You understand, don't you?"

"Sure. We kin do that. How'd you lose that eye, if you don't mind my asking?"

"I do mind. You two boys either sit with your brother or mount up and ride out of here. I asked you nice not to get on my blind side."

"Finn, you and Snooker set yourself down and try not to hurt this fellers feelings. We're the Linsky brothers from down near Franklinville. You ever heard of it?"

"Yes. I've heard of it. Even rode through there a couple of times."

"That sure is a good looking horse tied over there. You wouldn't want to sell or trade him, would you?"

"That'd be a foolish move for me to sell my horse, now wouldn't it?"

"I reckon I wasn't thinking straight."

I saw him reach down and touch the grip on his gun.

He fell back over the log he was sitting on. His brothers jumped to their feet brandishing their firearms. I hit the ground rolling out of the range and pulled off two quick shots, both hitting their mark. The brothers joined the oldest as they fell onto the hard ground.

"Lord, I hope you know I didn't have a choice. Is this what I'm going to be doing? I thought You wanted me to be a Preacher, not a killer?"

It was like I heard His voice loud and clear.

"Someone has to rid this land of the low life that inhabits it. You will have to be a Preacher and mete out whatever justice is necessary. This is what you were born to do."

"Heavenly Father. Did I understand correctly? I'm to be a Preacher and a killer? I thought I had left that kind of life behind me."

A calmness came over my body like it had back when I surrendered to preach. I remembered what Preacher said to me one time and I've said it to others many times.

"God don't make no mistakes."

"Alright, if that's what I'm to do, then so be it."

I pulled the three bodies out into the woods and located a pile of rocks. This would have to do. I covered them with as many rocks as I could find. Maybe that will keep the animals off for a while.

I walked back to camp, cleaned up the dishes, and rolled my bedroll. I brought Star over and saddled him. I gathered the reins of the men's horses, mounted up and took off again, riding this time away from the rising sun.

Two days later we came onto a small settlement. There wasn't a sign so I didn't know the name. There was a saloon, a store and five small buildings. Four horses were tied in front of the saloon.

I rode up, dismounted and tied Star between the other horses. I led the extra horses to the hitch post in front of the store and tied them there.

I walked back and entered the saloon. I stopped just inside the door to let my eye adjust to the darkness. Behind the bar was a small Mexican woman. She could barely see over the bar. Seated at a table were three drovers.

I walked over to the bar skirting around the table where the drovers were seated. When I turned back to the bar the woman was at eye level.

"I'm standing on a box. I saw your look of surprise."

"Didn't mean to stare, ma'am. You took me by surprise is all?"

"It happens all the time. What'll you have?"

"Just a glass of water, ma'am, I stopped drinking liquor a while back."

"I figured as much. You're a Preacher, ain't you?"

"Yes ma'am, I've been known to let loose with a few words."

"Just don't go feeding me none of that malarkey and we'll get along fine."

"I always try to please a beautiful young lady such as yourself."

"Ah. Go on now. Here's your water. If I might inquire, where you headed?"

"I don't rightly know that. I'm just trying to follow the path in front of me."

"Gets tiresome not knowing where you're going, don't it?"

"It could be, but then again, I meet some wonderful folks while I'm riding. Folks such as you, ma'am."

"There you go again. It ain't gonna do you no good."

"How's that, ma'am?"

"Trying to butter me up so's I'll listen to your spiel. Ain't interested."

"You have to give me credit for trying, don't you?"

"I can do that."

"Would there be someplace to get a bite to eat around here?"

"I reckon I can scare up a plate of stew if you're real hungry. I've not got many points in the cooking department."

"It would sure be appreciated, ma'am."

"Call me Kati, short for Katarina."

"I'll do that only if you call me Clint."

"Hello, Clint. I'll get that stew now."

She jumped down off the box and disappeared behind a curtain at the end of the bar.

"Did I hear you say you're a Preacher?"

"If you were listening, you did."

"I heard about a Preacher over in Silver Bluff that people say is a fast gun. I understand he's called the Pistol Preacher 'cause he carries a .45 something like yours. That wouldn't be you now, would it?"

"Depends on who's doing the asking."

"Don't get your drawers in a bunch. Just asking friendly like. We're just cow punchers from over at the Bar S about five miles south."

"Since you're asking nice, yes, I'm from Silver Bluff. I spent four years there, but now I on my way elsewhere."

"You know our Boss. Mr. Sweetson. Mr. Ralph Sweetson used to be real big on this church stuff, but he's laid up from a mean bronc throwing him a few years back. Doctor says he'll never walk or ride again. Reason I'm telling you this, is if you ain't got no place in particular to be, maybe you could ride back to the ranch with us and have a talk with him. He used to attend church regular 'afore this happened."

"How come some of you gents don't carry him to church in a wagon?"

"He says he don't want folks feeling sorry for him, so he just stays home."

"I'd be honored to travel with you gents. After I finish this delicious stew that Miss Kate has brought me."

"Why you want to punish your gut like that?"

"Hank, you better keep your mouth shut 'afore I shut it for you."

"Just kidding, Kate. Your stew is almost editable."

"You! Git yourself and your good for nothing friends outa my establishment. I didn't mean you, Clint."

"I'm going with these young rascals to visit their Boss. By the way, the stew was delicious. Goodbye until I see you again, lovely lady."

"Go on. Git outa here. You're too full of it. Bye."

CHAPTER FOURTEEN

I rode to the Bar S with the drovers. They were three of the happiest cowboys I had ever met. Hank, Lefty and Bruno. Apparently, Hank was a born leader because the others seemed to follow his lead in everything.

He was tall and thin. Had wavy brown hair, needed a trim. His clothes were typical cow puncher garb as were the others. They all had wide brimmed Stetsons.

Lefty, curly blonde hair was always chewing on a stick. Bruno, with a big round face and balding black hair was a big man, barrel chested, and always seemed to be frowning. Except when Hank would direct his words directly at him, then he would crack a smile.

The closer we came to the ranch, the boys seemed to quieten down and not say as much.

"Did you boys have permission to go off the reservation?"

"Oh, Mr. Sweetson don't care long as we get our work done. It's just that this time we didn't do everything he told us."

"Is that the real reason you wanted me to come back with you. Your boss isn't too keen on talking to a preacher, is he?"

"Well, he did kinda swear off anything to do with church. I reckon that would include Preachers, wouldn't it?"

"I tell you what. I believe God brought me here for a reason, so I'm ready for the challenge of meeting your boss. Lead the way."

We reached the main house which was a sprawling Ranch house. Made of Adobe and beautiful rock, brought up from South Texas in a wagon. As I said it was large. There were trees surrounding the building, creating shade all year round. We had just gotten off our mounts when, a loud booming voice shouted.

"You low down good for nothings. Get your scrawny butts in here. I didn't give you permission to go to that woman's saloon. Did I? I've told you a hundred times not to go there. If you've got to drink, go to town. At least they got some law there."

"We're sorry Boss. It won't happen agin. Say, we brought somebody to visit with you."

"Who would want to visit me? I sure don't want any visitors. Tell 'em to go away."

"Mr. Sweetson, my name's Clint Bowers and I'm a preacher. I understand that you're a Christian? Is that right?"

"Don't wanta talk about it. You need to ride back to wherever these scalawags found you. You boys go out and check the lower forty. I was told there was some cows crossing over a break in the fence. Now! Git outa here 'afore I git my gun."

I sat down on a chair on the other side of the room.

"I thought I told you to git?"

"I think you and I need to talk about your relationship with the Lord."

"Ain't got no relationship no more. Not since the accident."

"I don't think that's God's fault, is it? He's not the one that turned His back."

"If He loves His children, then why did He put me in this chair?"

"God's Word tells us He'll not put more on you than you can handle. I know you think this is the end of the world for you, but it's not. It's the beginning of a new life for you. The Bible also says that the trials that we have will only make us stronger. You believe the Bible, don't you?"

"Of course I believe the Bible. Everybody knows it's the Word of God. Even little kids know that."

"Then why aren't you accepting what it says?"

"I can't never walk or ride a horse again. Never."

"You may be in a chair, but your mind and your heart are very much able to do the work of God."

"How? When I'm stuck in this chair?"

"You could probably reach more people in that chair than you could sitting on top of a horse."

"How you figure that?"

"Well, one thing sitting up on a horse you'd be looking down on folks. In that chair you'd be level with them. They would tend to listen to you better."

"They're just gonna feel sorry for me, pity me."

"Only if you let them. If you act like a cripple, then folks will treat you like one. You're the same man you were before the accident. Your mind wasn't injured. Take control of your life with God's help and become a leader like you were before."

"Maybe you got some good points, but I'm still in this prison of a chair."

"It looks like it has wheels. You could probably go just about any place you want, maybe you'd need a little help in some places."

"I don't know. I just don't know. Do you really think I could?"

"Why don't we talk to the Lord about it? Would you like to do that?"

"I think I would. Will you pray with me, Preacher?"

"That's why I'm here. Let's bow our heads."

When we were through praying he looked at me.

"Would you come with me to church on Sunday? I'd like to introduce you to my friends."

"That sounds like a plan I can live with."

"Rosalita!" A middle aged Mexican woman poked her head around the door.

"Yes sir, Mr. Sweetson."

"Set another plate for the Preacher. You will eat with us?"

"I would be honored, thank you. I should probably look after my horse."

"If one of my hands hasn't already taken care of that, I'll be doing some more hollering."

CHAPTER FIFTEEN

I stayed with Mr. Sweetson the rest of the week. We had many talks and discussions about what God had done and was doing in our lives. He was very knowledgeable about the Word of God and we had a few heated discussions. But we both enjoyed the others company. Hank drove and I rode in the wagon with Ralph Sunday morning. It was probably fifteen miles to the church and it wasn't the best road. Lots of bumps, potholes and rocks. I know it was rough on him, but he didn't complain.

"I'm a little apprehensive about this."

"Don't worry. I'll be right beside you all the time. It's going to be alright."

"I hope you're right. There it is, up ahead. Don't look like much, but they're good people. Especially Widow Higgins. We had a thing before the accident. She's one fine woman."

"I'll be sure she's one of the first one's I meet." Hank pulled the wagon up as close as he could to the door.

"Hang on, Boss, I'm moving as fast as I can." As he jumped from the wagon seat and rushed back to help his Boss.

"Don't worry, Hank, I'm not going anyplace without some help." Hank and me lifted his chair out of the wagon and then up on the stoop.

"I think I'd like to try it on my own from here. Thanks, Hank. Preacher." He reached and started turning the wheels and navigated through the front door. The service had just started and they were singing. The Pastor was leading the people in song when Levi rolled through the door. He stopped in the middle of a verse. All eyes turned as one to see what he was looking at.

"There ain't nothing to look at. It's just me come to see my friends. Now get back to singing. I'm gonna sit right here at the end of this pew. Go on now. Sing." They began again with much more enthusiasm. At least it sounded that way to me. After the Pastor uttered the final prayer, folks rushed from their seats to welcome a lost sheep back into the fold. There was an older woman that seemed to be holding back, waiting for the others to move on.

"Preacher, I like you to meet Mrs. Mable Higgins. She came here from Philadelphia and opened a dress shop in town. She's a very special friend. Mable, this is Preacher. I done forgot your name."

"Clint Bowers, ma'am. Pleased to make your acquaintance. Ralph speaks highly of you."

"Please to meet you, Preacher. Anyone who could help Ralph is special in my eyes. Thank you, so much."

"You're most welcome. Now I'm going to check on the horses. I'll see you in a bit, Ralph." I left as she sat in the pew next to Ralph's chair. When I looked back they were holding hands. Mable's face was aglow with adoration. I was sure there'd be a wedding in the near future.

"I kind of enjoyed that, Preacher. Is it like this every Sunday?"

"Why don't you come back next Sunday and find out for yourself?"

"Well, the boys said they'd swap out days hauling the Boss to and from. But I may keep it to myself."

"Sounds like you did enjoy the service."

"Excuse me, Preacher." He took off and hurried over to a family loading the family into their wagon. I noticed they had a daughter about the same age as Hank. Maybe it wasn't only the service that caught his fancy.

I was leaning against the wagon admiring what the world looked like to young people, when the Pastor walked over to me.

"I missed meeting you when you came out of the church. I'm Reverend Josiah McCoggins. I can see you're a Preacher by the way you're dressed. Are you riding the circuit?"

"No. I just left my church in Silver Bluff in the care of an energetic young minister fresh out of the seminary. No. I'm not riding the circuit, although that doesn't sound like a bad idea. Do you know how a wondering Preacher might begin to do something like that?"

"I sure can. I rode the circuit for almost twenty years until I got too old to sit in the saddle. It was some of the happiest days of my ministry. Not that I'm not happy being a Pastor here. These are fine people. I wanted to thank you personally for helping Ralph Sweetson and convincing him to come back to church."

"I just explained to him that the path of life isn't always straight. Sometimes there are detours before we can get back on track. That's what happened to Ralph. He had a detour, but now he's headed in the right direction. I noticed Widow Higgins and he might be tying the knot anytime now."

"Yes, they were on that path, before the accident, and then when it happened, Ralph wouldn't talk to anyone, especially Mrs. Higgins. It's almost like he had injured not only his back, but his mind was somehow altered. Before it happened, he was one of the most congenial men around."

"I believe with God's help and perhaps a little help from his Pastor, he's going to be alright."

"Again, thank you so much. Ah. Here he comes. We'll be building a ramp before next Sunday, so it'll be easier to get him in and out of the building. How about you coming to visit day after tomorrow and we'll discuss how you can become a Circuit Riding Preacher. "

"I'm sure Ralph will appreciate the ramp, and I'll be here day after tomorrow, bright and early. Thank you."

Ralph rolled out onto the porch with Mrs. Higgins by his side.

"Hank! Tell the young lady goodbye and get over here. Your Boss is ready to go."

"That's ok, Preacher, I'm not in any hurry. Not anymore. I'm enjoying life too much. I'll see you later at the ranch, darling."

"I'll be there around six. Will that be alright?" She leaned down and brushed her lips across his forehead.

"That's perfect." He squeezed her hand, then turned our direction. "Ok, Hank. Preacher. Lift me off here and into that pesky wagon. I got plans to make."

"If I were to guess. Would that be wedding plans, Ralph?"

"Could be. Could be. You'll find out. Just wait. Have a little patience. Now, lift please?"

Both Ralph and Hank were in a very jovial mood on the ride back home. Not much was said. The three of us were deep in our own thoughts.

CHAPTER SIXTEEN

I bid farewell to the folks at the Circle J Ranch, with the promise that I would return, for the wedding between Ralph Sweetson and Mrs. Mable Higgins. No date had been set, but Ralph said it would probably be in the spring.

"It'll more than likely be in the spring. You just make arrangements no matter where you are to be here. I've already talked to Pastor McGoggins and he said it would be alright if we wanted you to join us in Holy Matrimony."

"I'll do that. I'll arrange my schedule for those dates to be open. But, if something urgent comes up and I can't make it back, please understand that I will be with you in spirit."

Hank came in the door. "Your horse is all saddled and I put some grub in your saddlebags that Rosalita fixed for you. Say Preacher, I want to thank you for making everything right with the Boss, and when you come back to marry him and the Widow, I might have some news for you."

"Are you getting serious about that young lady from church?"

"Her name is Heloise and I reckon I'm in love."

"Congratulations Hank, I wish you all the best. Will you tell the boys I said so long?"

"I'll do that. So long Preacher. I'm sure glad I met you."

"Likewise. Goodbye Ralph."

"Be seeing you Preacher."

I nodded and walked out the door, through the gate and climbed in the saddle. I pulled my hat down tight and gave Star his lead and we were off.

I rode back into town and went to see Pastor McCoggins for information about how to become a Circuit Riding Preacher.

We talked way into the night. He had all kinds of stories to tell about when he was riding the circuit. Some were sad, but most were of great victories that he had a part in.

"Since it's getting so late, why don't you bed down here tonight and get a fresh start in the morning."

"If you're sure I won't be a bother?"

"One more won't make much difference. Go on and put your horse in the barn. It's located to the right of the house."

"I'll do that. Be back in a jiffy." I went out and led Star to the barn, removed his saddle, brushed him a little and fed him a cup of grain. He was content chopping on his meal. I hoped the Pastor had something in mind to eat.

"You find everything ok?"

"Yes sir, thank you."

"I've got a covered dish that one of the ladies of the church brought over yesterday. You wanta try some? I'll have to heat it up a little."

"I was hoping for something like that. Do you need any help?"

"Sure, if you don't mind. Stick a couple pieces of wood in the stove and stir'em around a bit."

I picked up a couple pieces of wood and put them in the stove. Before long the fire caught and the reverend put the pot on the stove. The aroma smelled delicious. My stomach was talking back to me.

"Sounds like you're hungry. Grab a plate and spoon and dish out some of this. It's really good even if it is warmed over."

"If it tastes half as good as it smells, it'll be great. Um. You're right, it is good. If I might ask how long you been a widow?"

"Going on five years this September. That's the second wife. My first wife passed right after we were married. That's one of the reasons I started riding Circuit. I just couldn't seem to find any peace because of the loneliness. But traveling around the country, I was always meeting someone new. It got my mind off my loss."

"Is there a headquarters or someplace I need to check with before I start this journey?"

"There probably is, although I didn't worry about it. I only need one Boss telling me what to do and His Name is God."

"Sounds like a good plan. Thank you for the meal. It was very good. I think I'd like to turn in now. Like you said I need to get an early start in the morning. If you'll point me in the right direction, I'll say goodnight."

"Right through that door. There's a pitcher of water and a bowl for you to freshen up a bit. Goodnight Son."

CHAPTER SEVENTEEN

I saddled Star right after a couple of eggs, bacon and coffee. I bid Pastor McCoggins farewell and headed to the west. He had told me of a small town about fifty miles from here. I kicked Star into a gallop and we were off.

I had a funny feeling as I left the town that felt familiar. It felt like I had traveled this path before. It reminded me of my Bounty Hunting days. I suppose it was a little like it. The only difference was, now I'd be sending folks in a different direction for eternity.

Camping out under the stars was something I hadn't realized I missed so much until now. I would lay on my bedroll and watch the sky as it turned different colors. I could never understand how God put all this together, but I'm glad He did. It is a beautiful and wondrous sight to behold. The days were long and hot. Star and I stopped many times to rest in the shade of a big tree or some rock outcropping that would provide a little relief from the scorching sun.

I made camp beside a little rocky ledge. I built a small fire and made a pot of coffee. After watering Star and drinking a cup of coffee, I bedded down.

I had just woke up when I heard something that nobody wants to hear. The sound of a rattlesnake. I lay as still as possible. He sounded close. I couldn't see to my left because of my blind eye. If he was on that side and very close, I wouldn't be able to move until he decided to move on. I hoped I would be able to outlast him. I lay frozen to the ground very much afraid and with good reason.

"Hold still, stranger. I got a bead on'em, but he's laying right up against you. Probably hunting some shade from the morning sun. I'll try to work around to the other side. You lay still as you can. This time of year, they is mighty touchy. Ok. I'm gonna take my shot, but I need to tell you my eyesight ain't what it used to be."

I felt dirt spray over my face as the shot hit the snake. At least I hoped it hit the snake.

"Ok. You can relax. Man, he's a big one. You ever eat rattlesnake?"

"No. I never have. Thanks for showing up when you did, old timer. I thought I was a goner for sure."

"Name ain't Old Timer, Its Angus McTavish. I don't normally come this way. Just got a hankering I needed to change direction. Ain't that funny?"

"I'm Clint Bowers and I don't believe in coincidence."

"Coi what? Ain't never heard that one. What's it mean? Say yer a preacher ain't you?"

"I reckon I am. Coincidence means that nothing happens without a reason. I needed help and Someone changed your mind about which trail to take."

"You mean God made me come this way?"

"Yes, I believe that. So, you're a believer, too?"

"You can't survive out here without believing that the Almighty is running things."

"What are you doing out here, if I can ask?"

"Me and Gertrude, that's my mule over yonder a bit do a little trapping, a little huntin' and sometimes I find a nugget or two. Been doing it fer over sixty years I reckon."

"That's a long time. When's the last time you went to town?"

"Let me see. What year is it?"

"That long, huh?"

"It's been a spell alright. Where might you be headed?"

"I was told there's a small town around here someplace. You know anything about it?"

"Shore, there's a town yonder just over that little rise. Can't remember what name it goes by, but it's there ok."

"You want to join me in some bacon and beans?"

"You got any coffee. I ain't had no regular coffee in a month or Sundays. I'm gittin tired of chicory."

"I think I can scare up a cup for you since you're my hero."

"I ain't no hero. I just come along at the right time."

"And I'm mighty glad you did."

"I'll skin the rattler. You kin fry him up in the bacon grease. I ain't had none in a spell. Looking forward to enjoying it. You say you never had none, then you're in fer a treat."

"Are you sure you got all the poison out of it?"

"Ain't no poison on the inside. It's all in his mouth. I done cut his head off."

"I just put it in the skillet like bacon or chicken?"

"That's the way you do it."

I placed the first piece of fried rattlesnake onto a plate and handed it to Angus.

"Thank you. I'm gonna enjoy this." It had almost reached his mouth when there was a rifle shot and he fell forward into the fire. I grabbed him and pulled him out.

"Where you hit?" I didn't need to ask. My hand was covered with blood where the slug had exited out his back. There was no way he was gonna make it.

"I'm done fer. I stayed out in the open too long. Don't waste no more time on me. Go git him." The breath left his body and there wasn't another. I hurried to Star and threw the saddle on him. I jumped aboard and gave him a hup. I dug my boot heels into his side and flipped the reins. He jumped forward like something was chasing him. We topped the rise just as the man faded from sight. It would take some doing to catch him now. I pulled up on the reins and brought Star to a halt. I wiped my brow and put my hat back on.

"Good boy Star, you did fine. They were just too far ahead. We'll get'em next time." I turned Star back toward the camp. I felt bad for Angus. He was and always would be a hero in my mind. The least I could do is give him a proper burying. What was it he said about being out in the open too long? Was somebody chasing him or looking for him? Was he an outlaw? If he was, it had to have been a long time ago. He said he had been out here for sixty years.

I dug a grave with a flat piece of wood as best I could. I wrapped him in a blanket and placed his body in the makeshift grave. I pushed the dirt in on top of him and covered it with rocks to keep the animals from digging him up.

"Lord. I didn't know Angus very long, but what time we had together was real good. The man saved my life and claimed he was a believer. I pray that You've got a real fine mansion fixed up for him, because it doesn't look like he had much on this side. I ask for guidance for the days ahead and if You see fit, I'd kind of like to run into the man that shot Angus. Amen."

CHAPTER EIGHTEEN

Star and I rode into the small town of Brazos Branch, Texas. I suppose they named it that because of being located along the banks of the Brazos River. It was filled with green trees and green grass. It didn't look as though they were hurting for water. The town proper had a few businesses along the Main Street of the town. I saw a saloon of course, a general store, a telegraph office, a barber shop, a bakery and at the end of the street the building I was looking for. The livery stable.

"Welcome, stranger. Unravel and climb down. I'll take good care of your horse. He's a beauty ain't he?"

"Can you tell me if there's a church in town?"

"I figured you might be a Preacher, way you're dressed. There's one out past the old train station. Ain't got no train no more. Ain't enough people, so's they say. Same amount when they built it. Church's been empty since the preacher got hisself killed trying to break up a gunfight. Though it was kind of foolish fer him to do it, but it weren't none of my business. You figuring on preaching in that church are you? Name's Archie Garrety. He was a redheaded man with a robust belly, wearing leather trousers, a stained light brown shirt. On top of his red hair was a ship captain's cap. This here's my stable. How long you figuring on staying?"

"I'm Clint Bowers, but most everybody calls me Preacher."

"I heared that name before. Bowers. Say you're not that Pistol Preacher are you? The one shot and killed that fellow, Link Baxter? They say he was the fastest man alive. And yet here you stand living and breathing. I'm real honored to make your acquaintance. Preacher."

"Take good care of my horse, please."

"Sure thing. I'll give an extra scoop of grain. You headed to the church?"

"I thought I might get a bite to eat first. Where might I do that?"

"Only place is the saloon. It ain't the best grub, but it's filling. Tell Francis I sent you."

"Francis being a gent or a lady?"

"Oh Francis is a man and very much so. You'll see when you meet him."

I walked past the other businesses and went into the saloon. There were six tables filled with all different types of men. Most were dressed in drover's outfits. A couple dressed as shopkeepers. Behind the bar was perhaps the biggest man I had ever seen. He stood easily over six feet seven inches. His chest was enormous, stretching his shirt almost popping the buttons. His head was as bald and as big as a pumpkin. He had a round shiny face with shiny white teeth sporting a white spade beard.

"Welcome. Come on in stranger, what'll it be?"

"You Francis?"

"Could be. Who's doing the asking?"

"Garrety told me to look you up. Said you might could fill this gnawing stomach of mine."
"Name's Francis Fontecchio. You don't need no special introduction from that no good if you're hungry. Got some Italian goulash in the back. You can go back there or you can eat here at the bar, since there ain't no empty chairs. Got a full house tonight. Happens like this every Friday night. All the cowboys come to town to raise a ruckus."

"If it's ok, I'll eat in the back. I need to rest my back. Been in the saddle all day."

"Do you happen to know a fellow by the name of Angus McTavish?"

"I've heard of him. Don't know the man personally, but it's strange you should ask. A man was in here two or three days ago asking that same question."

"Could you describe the man?"

"Sure. Why don't you go on in the back and get a plate of goulash. I'll be back in a minute or two and we'll talk."

"Sounds good."

"Tell my old woman I sent you back. She's a little fussy about who goes in her kitchen."

"She's not going to stick a knife in me, is she?"

"Just tell her I said you're ok." I parted the curtains separating the rooms and went into the back room.

"What'cha doing in my kitchen?" She was short, maybe an even five feet, her back stooped with age. White hair with streaks of black running through it, wearing a pale blue dress and apron that matched. And she had a meat cleaver in her hand.

"Francis said I could come back here for a plate of your delicious goulash. Would you mind? I haven't eaten since morning."

"If the old man said it's ok, then I reckon it's ok. Set yourself down. I'll get you a plate."

"Thank you kindly, ma'am."

Francis came in and sat down across from me

"Can't let Rodriguez tend bar by himself too long. He starts giving away free drinks. Bring me a cup of coffee Old Woman and bring some bread for Clint to go with the goulash." She laid a half loaf of bread on the table with a knife.

"You ain't helpless, get your own coffee. It's right there on the stove." He poured a cup for himself and one for me.

"That fellow asking about McTavish called himself, Moss or Mose, something like that. Really didn't pay that much attention. I will say he wasn't overly friendly."

"How's that?"

"Had a sneer on his face. Looked like it was froze that way. Didn't crack a smile the whole time he was here. Didn't want nothing to do with the fairer sex neither."

"Did he say why he was looking for McTavish?"

"Nope. Just asked if I knew him, downed his beer and left."

"You happen to see which direction or what his horse looked like?"

"Nope."

"Say this goulash isn't bad. You called it Italian goulash?"

"Yeah. My old woman's from Italy. Came over on a boat back in 32 with her parents. I met her on a trip to New York to get furniture for a salon I was going to build in Ft Worth. Lost it all on the turn of a card. Swore off gambling then and there. Fellow grubstaked me and here I am. In this God forsaken Texas no man's land."

"Come on now. You know you like Texas."

"Yeah. I reckon I'm a Texan alright. Wouldn't want to live no place else. Can't say the same for the old woman. She hates it here. But she says it's for better or worse. That's what she signed up for."

"Maybe she could go back east and visit her folks?"

"Her folks been dead going on ten years. She wanted to go back before they was gone, but I didn't have no money. Reckon she's going to hold it against till I'm dead and gone."

"Where's a place to bed down for the night? I'm plumb tuckered out."

"Got an empty room upstairs. Reckon you can have it. Seeing as how you're a Preacher and all."

"You sure are being kind to a stranger."

"Don't consider a saddlebag Preacher a stranger. You figuring on preaching Sunday morning?"

"I thought I might say a few words if the church is fit to hold a meeting."

"It ain't. You can hold your meeting here in the saloon. Boys can do without their liquor for one day. Come next Sunday if you're still here, the church will be cleaned and ready. It's been a spell since there was a man of God here. I'm looking forward to hearing what you got to say."

"I hope you're not disappointed. I thank you for the use of your business and for fixing up the church building. I'll probably stick around for a couple of days, maybe more. Depends on what the Lord has planned for me. Now, if you'll excuse me, I believe I'll hit the hay.

Thank you, ma'am, the goulash was delicious. Good night to you both."

"Goodnight Preacher. Have a restful night."

CHAPTER NINETEEN

I woke the next morning to a bright hot Texas sun. It was stifling in the room. I looked out the window and I could see the heat bouncing off the hard dirt. I walked downstairs. Francis was behind the bar.

"Top of the morning to you Preacher. I trust you had a restful night."

"Morning Francis. You think I could talk your wife into a couple of eggs this morning?"

"Sure thing. I done told her you was to get special treatment as long as you're here. Go on back."

"Good morning Mrs. Fontecchio. If it's not too much trouble, could you fry me a couple eggs with some bacon?"

"My old man tells me you're a Preacher, is that right?"

"Yes ma'am, that's right."

"I'll fix anything you want, you being a Preacher and all."

"Thank you, ma'am. May I ask if there's a river or lake close by. I need to wash off some of this trail dust?"

"There's a small pond just east of here. You need to be leery of snakes though. They're plentiful this time of year. About half a mile, I reckon. How you want these eggs?"

After breakfast, I saddled Star and headed east. I came on the spot Mrs. Fontecchio told me about.

Located in a small canyon, it wasn't a lake, just a big pothole where the water collected before it overflowed and ran on down to the main branch of the river. It was out of the way and a good place for hiding from someone looking for you. I sat on the grassy bank inhaling the scent of wildflowers and the cedar trees surrounding this hideaway. There wasn't a lot of sunlight, so the mosquitoes and dragonflies were flying all around. I kept swatting to no avail. I don't know if the coolness of the pond was worth all the trouble. Maybe I would go further upriver and find a place that wasn't inhabited by so many small creatures. I mounted Star and started following the runoff. As I cleared the overhanging branches, I glanced up at the brilliant blue sky with streaks of yellow where the sun was filtering through the clouds. The sound of an eagle broke the silence. I rode out of the canyon as the sun came from hiding behind a cloud. It illuminated every rock, every hill and plant. It was a glorious sight to see.

"Thank You, Lord for bringing me to this place where I have new friends and beautiful scenery. I ask for Your continued blessing and guidance as I do Your work. Amen."

We were still following the runoff looking for the main river, when a rifle shot whizzed by my ear. It was on my blind side so it took a while for me to adjust my vision. I jumped from the saddle, settled behind a rock, and scanned the bushes all around. Another shot barely missing my leg, which was sticking out from my cover. I jerked it up close to me and raised up just enough to take another look. There he was, about a hundred yards away, up on a big rock holding a rifle. He was sitting there in the open figuring he was safe because he was out of range for my .45.

I was going to have to figure a way to move closer if I had any chance at all. I took careful aim and squeezed the trigger. Dirt flew up just to the bottom of his perch.

I turned and looked all around. He had sure picked a good spot for an ambush. I couldn't see any way of escape.

Then I remembered something Cotton had told me.

"The Colt.45 Peacemaker is a very remarkable weapon. Because of its longer barrel, it can shoot farther than the normal barrel. You just have to aim your shot a little higher."

I raised up, placed my arm on the rock for support. I aimed about a foot above the vermin's head and squeezed the trigger. He jerked as the slug hit him. He dropped the rifle, grabbed his chest and tumbled off the rock all the way to the ground.

I stood, walked over where he was laying. He was still alive.

"You're not going to make it, partner, so why not go out clean. What's your name and why were you shooting at me?"

"Name's Moses Kildane. You was with McTavish when I shot him. Can't have no witnesses to tell the sheriff about me."

"Why'd you kill McTavish?"

"He killed my Pa fifteen years ago down in south Texas. Couldn't look for him until I got old enough, then it took a long time to find him."

"You want to ask God to accept you into His kingdom while there's still time?"

"There ain't no God in my life. Ain't been for a long time. I don't figure there's a Heaven or a hell. If there is, I'll accept whichever way I slide." With those last words he left this world.

I lifted him up onto his horse, retrieved Star and rode back to the settlement of Brazos Branch. I stopped at the livery stable.

"This the fellow killed McTavish?"

"Yes, he confessed to it, before he died. There's not an undertaker here, is there?"

"Nope, but there's a cemetery off yonder on that rise. Olan Pickett takes care of it. He'll bury the gent if you ride him over. Pickett lives in a little shack near the cemetery. You can't miss it."

"Thanks. I'll take him over now."

I rode over to the cemetery and made arrangements for Pickett to dig the grave for Kildane.

"I'll be over a little later to say some words for the deceased."

"Sure thing Preacher. I'll get everything ready and wait on you before I cover the grave."

"Thank you." I rode Star back to the livery stable.

"You find Pickett ok?"

"Yes. Everything's taken care of."

"Sure thing. You going back to the saloon are you?"

"So long."

I led Star down the street and tied him up in front of the saloon.

"You have a nice soak in that little pond?"

"Didn't get the chance. I met the man that shot McTavish."

Did you have a talk with him?" "Yes, we talked after a bit. He tried the same thing with me that he did with McTavish."

"I see he wasn't successful."

"No. But it was close. He almost got me."

"I'm sure glad. I'd hate to have to wait for another Preacher to show up here."

Star and I went back to the spot where I was ambushed and continued toward the main branch of the Brazos River. We found just the spot. It was about two feet deep with a dark green grassy bank. I loosened Star's cinch and let him start munching the lush greenery. I removed my clothes and waded into the cool clear water. I sat down flat. What a luscious feeling. My tense muscles began relaxing as the water moved across my body. I spent probably an hour soaking in that marvelous place. I finally got up, dried off and dressed in clean clothes. I felt a hundred percent better.

CHAPTER TWENTY

I stayed in Brazos Branch for two weeks. It was an enjoyable time, spent with good friends. The church was filled with folks from near and far. Now it was time for me to move on. A Circuit Rider isn't supposed to grow roots in the first place he comes to. There are other towns and settlements that need the Word of God.

"Clint, you know you've got have a permanent place here with us?"

"I know and I appreciate that, but I feel God is calling me elsewhere. I have faith that the Lord will send another preacher along any day now. You can lead the church until then. You are a deacon now."

"I don't know how I let you talk me into that."

"You can't fool me. You like the idea of the responsibility."

"You could be right. I do at that. Where you headed from here?"

"I'll flick Star's reins and follow wherever he takes me. So long good friend. If I don't see you again on this side, I'll see you in the next. Goodbye, Mrs. Fontecchio. You've got a good man here."

"Don't tell him, but I agree. Goodbye, Preacher. May you travel with the angel's wings protecting you?"

I travel from town to town preaching about the love of God to any and all that will listen.

It's a hard road to travel, always checking your back trail only to find that trouble is waiting for you when you arrive at your destination.

They call me The Pistol Preacher.

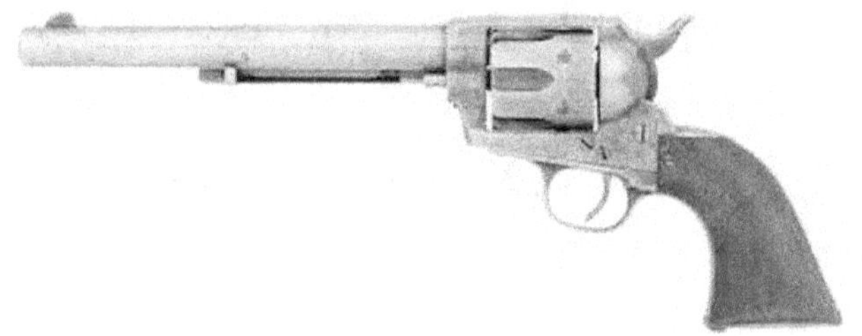

Other Books by J.C. Hulsey

Angel Falls, Texas
Velvet Sky, Arizona
Angry Orchard, Colorado
Clear Stone, Wyoming
Itching Tree, Idaho
Windy Butte, New Mexico
Devil's Dance, Dakota Territory
Redemption Road
Red Rose
Rebecca
The Concho Kid
Ugly Mugly
GUTSHOT
The Last Ride
The Old Man
The Pistol Preacher
Shortland
Dynamite
The Concho Kid
Dead Man's Gun
Does Nora Know
Doke Walker
Brothers
Satan's Refuge
Shadrack
The Brute
The Decision
The Greenhorn
The Gunfight
The Hangman

www.ingramcontent.com/pod-product-compliance
Lightning Source LLC
Chambersburg PA
CBHW071333140726

47996CB00005B/1948